Cinnamon Lake Mysteries

Don't Bug Me, Molly!

Dandi Daley Mackall
Illustrated by Kay Salem

CPH.
SAINT LOUIS

To my mom.
Thanks for putting up with all our pets
all those years.

Copyright © 1997 Dandi Daley Mackall
Published by Concordia Publishing House
3558 S. Jefferson Avenue, St. Louis, MO 63118-3968
Manufactured in the United States of America

Library of Congress Cataloging-in-Publication Data

Mackall, Dandi Daley.
        Don't bug me, Molly!/Dandi Daley Mackall; illustrated by Kay Salem.
            p.   cm.—(Cinnamon Lake mysteries)
        Summary: The mysterious behavior of Sunny Miller, a Korean adopted
into an American family in Cinnamon Lake, involves Molly and the gang
in a case of bug burglars, stage fright, and Jesus' love.
        ISBN 0-570-04884-2
        [1. Korean Americans—Fiction. 2. Christian life—Fiction. 3. Mystery and
detective stories.] I. Salem, Kay, ill. II. Title. III. Series.
        PZ7.M1905Do 1997
        [Fic]—dc21   96-39174

1 2 3 4 5 6 7 8 9 10   06 05 04 03 02 01 00 99 98 97

97-1539

Cinnamon Lake Mysteries

The Secret Society of the Left Hand
The Case of the Disappearing Dirt
The Great Meow Mystery
Don't Bug Me, Molly!

*I'm not sure how we got famous
as the Cinnamon Lake Mystery Club.
I mean, the Cinnamon Lake part
is easy. That's where we live.
The mystery part is more ...
mysterious.*

Contents

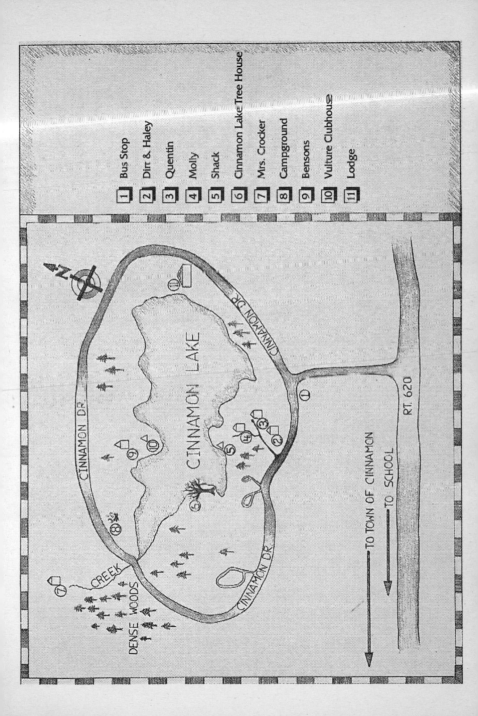

1 Bus Stop
2 Dirr & Haley
3 Quentin
4 Molly
5 Shack
6 Cinnamon Lake Tree House
7 Mrs. Crocker
8 Campground
9 Bensons
10 Vulture Clubhouse
11 Lodge

1

A Ghost of a Chance

"*Ah-hhhh!* It's a ghost!" Haley's scream hung over the lake. She grabbed my arm so tight it hurt.

"What's the matter with you, Haley?" I said, trying to jerk my arm back.

"Right there, Molly Mack!" Haley screamed so close to my eardrum her words pounded in my head.

We were deep in the woods, taking the shortcut to our Cinnamon Lake tree house. The sun had gone down fast, and now the moon provided our only light.

"There it is again!" Haley yelled, pointing toward Cinnamon Lake.

I squinted in the direction Haley pointed. "There's no such thing as ghosts, Haley," I said.

Then I saw it. In the old shack at the edge of the lake, something moved.

"I'm getting out of here!" Haley whined.

My heart pounded, even though I didn't believe in ghosts. "Haley," I said, "We're third-graders, not kindergartners. We *know* there aren't ghosts."

The moonlight stretched fingers to the broken-down shack, as if pointing out the holes and cracks. I looked again. A shadow moved across the broken window. "You win!" I said. "Let's get out of here!"

We tore through the woods, stumbling over tree stumps and fallen logs. Branches snapped. Haley ran in front of me, her long, dark hair flying like it had a life all its own. She ran through low branches. One slapped me in the face and made my eyes water.

At last we reached our Cinnamon Lake tree house. Quentin and Dirt were already there. We don't have a house in our tree yet, but it's the best tree in all Cinnamon Lake. Never was I more glad to see it! I climbed to my branch, the highest. Haley scrambled past her branch, the lowest.

"Hey!" Dirt yelled. "Off my branch! What's with you? You look like you've seen a ghost."

Dirt is Haley's little sister, two years younger, and a full member of our Cinnamon Lake Club. Dirt is the toughest first-grader in the world.

"We *have* seen a ghost!" Haley whined, panting as she held her ground on Dirt's branch. "Down by that old haunted shack. We barely made it out of the woods alive!"

Quentin made a disapproving clucking noise. He shook his head at Haley. Quentin is round and short. His legs stuck straight out from the tree branch. "How many times have I told you, Haley?" he said, sounding much older than a third-grader. "There are no such things as ghosts. Now, repeat it with me. *There are no such things as ghosts.*"

Haley didn't repeat it. "Repeat it yourself, Quentin," she said. "There was too a ghost. Just ask Molly!"

All heads turned to me. In the dark, Quentin looked like a shadowy clay figure. "Molly?" he said.

"Well, we did see something," I said weakly.

"Far out!" Dirt said. "Like where?"

"Down by that old haunt—, er, old shack," I said.

"Nonsense," Quentin said. "It is only your imagination."

"No, Quentin," I said. "I saw something ... or someone."

"See?" Haley said, sounding smug.

"I get my lightning bugs by that shack," Dirt said. She stood on her branch like a tightrope walker. "I'll bet you saw lightning bugs. Or moths. Some of those moths throw a mean shadow."

"Maybe," I said. But I knew better.

"Want me to check it out with you?" Dirt asked.

"Yeah, that would be great!" I said. "Tomorrow?" I didn't want to face whatever was down there in the dark.

Quentin cleared his throat. It sounded a little like the frogs croaking all around us. Our tree had so much spring growth, some of the branches reached right over Cinnamon Lake. The air had a damp smell to it.

"Honestly, Molly," Quentin said. "I would think you have enough to worry about with the science fair just around the corner. Use your imagination on the fair, instead of on Haley's ghost."

Quentin was right—as usual. I hadn't thought of much else since Mr. Adams told us we'd all have to present a project for a Junior Science Fair Day at our school. My throat dried up every time I thought about it.

"I can't wait for the fair!" Haley said. "I'll be showing all of Aunt Mary's doll collection. And my dress will match her prize doll's dress."

"Very scientific," Quentin muttered.

Then Haley looked up at me. "How are *you* ever going to present a project in front of the whole school? You get tongue-tied when you have to answer a question in Mr. Adams' class."

I shrugged. I had asked myself that same question about a million times.

"My gray cells have been working night and day," said Quentin. That's what he calls thinking. "My only problem will be convincing the judges that a third-grader, myself, was the only scientist behind my project."

Besides the science fair talk, we didn't have much Cinnamon Lake business. We complained about the Vultures for a while. They have a real club house on the other side of the lake. Their goal in life is to ruin anything we try to do.

"I move we adjourn," Quentin said. "I can still get in a couple of hours on my science experiment."

Dirt jumped straight down from her branch. She landed on both feet, then did a somersault. Quentin and Haley climbed down backwards. I was the last one down. Haley, Quentin, and I headed toward Cinnamon Drive. Dirt took off to the deeper part of the woods—probably to feed bats or raccoons.

We were almost to the place where Haley and I had seen her "ghost." It was darker now. I could barely make out the shack down by the lake.

I heard Haley whispering to herself, "There are no such things as ghosts. There are no such things as ghosts."

The crickets chirped louder. The tips of the pines swayed in the wind as if they were sweeping the stars from the sky.

We were halfway up the hill from the shack when something jumped out of the bushes. All three of us screamed! Haley grabbed me from behind and hid her head in my back. We stood there, frozen.

"*AAAaaa—oooo,*" came a spine-tingling howl. Then another, "*Yaaaa-eeeee.*" We kept still, hoping whatever it was couldn't see us.

From behind us came loud laughter, and out of the bushes jumped Sam and Ben Benson. Vultures! Sam is in third grade, like Quentin, and Haley, and me. He's not quite as mean as his brother, Ben. Ben is a fifth-grader who looks like an eighth-grader, but acts like a preschooler.

"That's not funny!" I said, trying to keep my voice from shaking.

"My, aren't we amusing," Quentin said.

"Yep!" Sam said. "Very amusing." His red hair fell across his forehead as he shook with laughter.

"We thought you were the ghost—" Haley said, before I could stop her.

"Ridiculous," Quentin muttered. "Ghosts are scientifically impossible."

"You mean the ghost in that shack?" Ben asked, pointing to the lake.

"You know the ghost?" Haley asked.

"Beware of the Ghost of the Haunted Shack," Ben said in a low, scary voice.

"Don't listen to him, Haley," I said. "You know ghosts aren't real."

"Oh, yeah?" Sam said, pointing. "Then what's that?"

In the broken window of the old shack, I could see the outline of a person. The figure paced back and forth, a candle glowing in its hand.

"Let's get out of here!" Haley cried. And we all took off running.

We scattered in every direction, like blackbirds scared out of a cornfield. I'm much more of a tomboy than Haley, but I was no match for her terror. I had to run hard to keep up with her. I don't know what's happening, Jesus, I prayed, but keep us safe.

Behind me, I heard Quentin and Sam. But I didn't look back. I felt that if I looked back, something awful would happen. I'd turn into a pillar of salt, maybe, like Lot's wife. There was no doubt about it.

Something was in that shack.

2

Sunny-side Up

"Okay," Mr. Adams said, taking off his glasses and leaning back on his big desk. Our teacher is so thin. He reminds me of those rubber figures you can bend and knot. "Let's finish up our newspaper reports," he said. "Who's left?"

I traced cracks in my desk with my finger and tried to look invisible.

"Molly hasn't done hers yet," Sam Benson said.

I glared at Sam. He winked back at me. I hated this assignment a hundred times worse than anything. Each week we were supposed to clip an article out of the newspaper and report to the class.

"Molly?" Mr. Adams said. "Looks like you're up."

I pulled my crumpled newspaper article out of my desk and smoothed out some of the wrinkles. I kept rubbing my hand over it until Mr. Adams came and stood by my desk.

"Better stand up and face the class," he said.

I felt like I was facing a firing squad.

"We're waiting, Molly," he said.

I knew that. I was waiting too. For lightning. For a tornado. For a fire drill. Anything.

I got to my feet, which wasn't easy, since my legs felt like they had Jell-O for bones. I swallowed hard. I prayed that if God didn't choose now for a fire drill, He'd at least help me say something that wasn't too stupid. I took a deep breath and read my headline. *"Wildlife Threat Comes to Cinnamon Lake."*

"A little louder, will you, Molly?" Mr. Adams asked. He walked back to his desk.

I leaned one hand on my desk and looked down at the article. Why hadn't I taken more time to brush my hair? It was as if I just realized I needed a haircut. Blonde strands of hair flopped in my face. I pushed them behind my ears.

I repeated the title. Maybe it was louder. But the buzzing in my ears was so loud, I couldn't hear my own words. "Cinnamon Lake is home to a lot of geese and birds."

I looked up. Most kids seemed to be listening. Maybe I could get through this. "Um ... We all love to hear the geese. You know, when they fly over Cinnamon and stop at Cinnamon Lake on their way to warmer lands in the winter. But some people are trying to get rid of the geese. They want to make money off Cinnamon Lake." I was stammering on some of the words, but the worst was over. I was doing it!

Then everything changed. First I saw Sam turn his back on me. Whispers broke out all over the room. I looked at Quentin, but he was staring at the back of the room too. Everybody was turning around toward the door.

"Go on, Molly," Mr. Adams said.

But it was hard talking to the backs of kids' heads. "A land developer," I said. But the words felt like they were trying to break out of jail. Sounds pushed at the bars of my teeth to get out. I couldn't remember what to say next. Nobody was listening anyway.

"Oh, I didn't see you!" Mr. Adams called to someone outside the door, in back of the room where I couldn't see. "Please, come on in."

I stood there, my mouth still open, my unfinished article crumpled again in my fist. In walked a tall, slender girl with straight black hair and dark brown eyes. She looked like a princess of the Orient. Like someone you'd read about in books about China or Korea. She wore designer jeans, earrings that looked like red diamonds, a silky red blouse, and a quilted vest.

I rubbed the toe of my dirty gym shoes on the back of my worn jeans and wished I'd worn a nicer T-shirt.

"Please, come in. Find a seat," Mr. Adams said. He met her halfway and put his hand on her shoulder. "Class," he said. "I'd like you to meet a new student ... uh ..."

"Sunny," she said. Instead of being embarrassed out of her mind like I would have been, she smiled to the class and greeted us. I had kind of expected her to have a quiet, soft accent. Instead, in a loud, clear, 100 percent American voice, she said, "I'm glad to meet you. I'm sure I will love your beautiful Cinnamon Lake."

Mr. Adams glanced around the room. "Let's see. You'll need a desk, Sunny. For now, you can sit back there. Then we'll see if we can't get you closer to the board."

"Great," Sunny said, taking the only empty seat.

"Would someone agree to switch desks with Sunny at recess?" Mr. Adams asked. "She needs front-row seating."

You get dibs on front-row desks if you have trouble hearing the teacher or seeing the board. She wasn't wearing glasses or hearing aids. Maybe contacts. *I* had earned my front-row seat for passing notes when I wasn't supposed to.

"I'll switch," I said. But just as I said it, I realized what I was saying! That other desk. It was right between Sam Benson and Caleb Twig! Talk about a fate worse than death.

"Great!" Mr. Adams said. "So, Sunny, you can move your things up here after recess. Now then. Where were we?"

I had slipped into my seat, hoping Mr. Adams would forget about my article.

"Molly?" Mr. Adams called. "Finish your report, please."

My article was crumpled in my sweaty hand. I couldn't remember what I'd said or what I should say. Everybody was looking at the new girl anyway. My neck felt so tight, I couldn't imagine getting words through it and out my mouth.

I opened my mouth, but nothing came out. It got so quiet, I could hear my heart beat. What was the article about? Geese. Somebody threatening the geese.

"Uh ..." I had to say something so I could sit down, even if I had to sit between Sam and Caleb. "Some rich land developer wants to kill off the geese," I said.

The new girl looked straight up at me, as if I'd done something to her. Then she stared down at her desk.

I slunk down in my seat as far as I could go. Something about that new kid made me want to go home.

3

Knock, Knock!
Who's There?

"Follow me and stay low," Dirt whispered. She had on a rain poncho the color of leaves at night. I wished I'd worn mine. The mist was thick enough to feel like rain. Dirt crouched a lot lower than I could get.

We were in the woods, a little farther from the shack than Haley and I had walked the night before. A half moon gave us enough light to see to the lake. I hoped there wasn't enough light to be seen by whoever was in that shack. I clicked on my flashlight.

"Turn that thing off!" Dirt barked. "You want to give us away?"

"I want to know what I'm stepping on," I said. I tried to turn the light off. It was one of the flashlights Dad got from work. He makes up slogans for all kinds of companies. And sometimes they give him free products. His slogan was on this company's flashlights: *Barney's Carpet City—Throw a Whole New Light on Your Rug!*

I finally got it turned off.

"Close your eyes. Count to ten. Then open them. You can see better by the moonlight," Dirt said.

"Do you see anybody?" I whispered. I closed my eyes, counted, then opened them. Dirt was right.

"*Shhh!*" Dirt moved in closer to the shack. Even I couldn't hear her move. I tiptoed after her, sounding like a herd of elephants compared to Dirt. We took a spot behind a maple tree so thick with green leaves I felt safe. Rain dripped from the leaves and made my sweatshirt stick to me. A shiver went down my spine.

The moon shone off the water, through the shack window, and then to us. I could just see inside the shack. "I think it's empty," I said.

Dirt didn't answer. Instead, before I knew she was gone, she'd slithered all the way to the window! She grabbed the window ledge with both hands, and with her chin on the sill, peered inside!

"Dirt? Is the coast clear?" I called.

Without turning around, she motioned with one arm for me to come.

I came. But before I got there, she had rolled to the side of the shed, turned the corner, and disappeared! Then I couldn't see or hear Dirt—only an owl, and a chorus of frogs and crickets.

I crouched below the window, leaning against the wall, breathing hard. What if whoever was in the shed had captured Dirt? What if they were waiting for me? What if—

"Boo!" Dirt stuck her head through the window from inside the shed.

I jerked back! My head bumped the windowsill and knocked me to the ground. Wet weeds grabbed at my jeans.

"It's cool, Molly," Dirt said. "You can use the door."

I picked myself up and walked around to the door. Inside it was too dark to see anything. I dug my flashlight out of my jeans pocket and turned it on. Dirt didn't object.

"That one of your dad's flashlights?" she asked.

"Throw a whole new light on your rug," I said in my radio announcer voice.

"Make your mark," Dirt said in her radio voice. That was Dad's pencil slogan for the pencil factory. We had a zillion of those pencils lying around.

I shined the light straight in front of me. There was a crate that held five or six glass jars, each about half full of dirt. Next to it was a stump somebody probably used as a chair. A shovel leaned against one wall.

"Shine it over here!" Dirt said. "Look! Clothes!"

In the beam of light we could see old sweat pants that would have fit me and a couple of shirts.

"Yuk! These are gross!" I said. The sweats were caked in dried mud. "I'll bet some poor homeless person is staying here. Maybe we should leave stuff for him, like food and clean clothes."

On one side of the shed, the farthest from the door, several big boxes were stacked. Dirt was already going through them. "What did you find?" I asked, joining her.

"Man!" Dirt said in a long, low voice.

I peeked in the box. "Toaster?" I asked.

Dirt took out a wad of newspaper and unrolled it. "Silverware!" she said, holding up a spoon. "I think it's the real stuff."

There was one big box, but it was empty except for squashed paper cups. I checked out another box. "Now, why do you suppose he—?" I started. Dirt threw her hand over my mouth so hard it felt like a slap!

"Hey!" My protest was muffled by Dirt's grubby hand. With her other hand she pushed me into the biggest box. She grabbed the flashlight out of my hand and switched it off. Then Dirt jumped in the box on top of me. It was all I could do not to let out a moan. I tried to keep still, but Dirt's bare foot was two inches from my nose.

Then I heard it. At first, it was just a rustling of leaves. It might have been the wind. It might have been one of the millions of squirrels or raccoons that make Cinnamon Lake their home. But Dirt wouldn't have shoved me inside a box for a raccoon.

A twig broke. There was shuffling on the path outside. The door to the shack creaked. And then it was flung open! Somebody—or something—was inside the shack with us.

4

Close Call

I was lying on my side, curled up in the bottom of a cardboard box. Dirt's big toe poked me in the eye. I shoved it away. I held my breath and prayed. I found myself thinking, *The Lord is my Shepherd. I shall not want. He makes me lie down in green pastures.* I felt better, remembering God was there with Dirt and me inside a box inside a shack. But I wished we were in a green pasture instead.

A drawer slammed. I heard footsteps. A long scraping sound—the stump being pulled back? Why had we come to the shack? What had I been thinking of? I had to get home ... in one piece.

Dirt made no noise at all. It was like she'd stopped breathing.

The stump screeched again. Then there were other noises. A low grunting sound. Somebody moving, but staying in one place. Something dropped. Then something else plunked to the ground.

Footsteps crossed the floor. Somebody was walking toward the door. Maybe they were leaving! Maybe ... But they stopped. And I heard the footsteps coming back. *Click, click, clunk.* Like a wooden leg, or a cane now. The steps got closer. *Click, click, clunk.*

Closer and closer. Something bumped the side of the box. I squeezed my eyes shut, as if that would make whatever was out there blind. It seemed we stayed like that, frozen, until I couldn't take it anymore. My throat tickled. I had to cough. I tried to swallow, but there wasn't anything to swallow. Or what was there was blocked by a huge lump.

Then the footsteps quickly crossed the shack and faded away. Dirt didn't move. I didn't move.

Still no sounds except an owl in the distance and a cricket inside the shack. "Dirt?" I said softly. No answer.

"Dirt?" I said louder, suddenly afraid something had happened to her.

Dirt popped out of that box like she was a jack-in-the-box. I felt both of her bare feet on my head.

"Ow!" I cried. I peeked over the side of the box. A stream of light poured through the open door of the shack. I climbed out. "Let's get out of here, Dirt," I said. I started for the door, but I stumbled over something. "What—?"

Clothes were thrown across the floor. Clean blue jeans lay in the path of moonlight.

"Dirty clothes are gone," Dirt said. "And the shovel."

"So that's what the clink, clink, clunk was," I whispered. "Footsteps and a shovel!" But I didn't feel like hanging around and solving the mystery. "Dirt," I said. "Let's get out of here before he comes back."

Dirt got to the door ahead of me. She looked both ways, crouched, and crept back the way we came. I was right beside her. I never looked back.

The next morning I could hardly wait to talk to Dirt. I got to the bus stop later than

usual. Dirt was giving her daily morning warning: "Fifth grade alert!"

That meant Ben Benson or Marty or one of the other Vultures was in sight. About 10 kids huddled together like for a tornado drill. I joined them. "Dirt," I said. "We have to talk about last night."

"You tell your folks?" she asked. Her jeans and white T-shirt looked like she'd slept in them.

"They're not back yet," I said. "Mom's conference isn't over until Saturday. I didn't want to worry Granny."

My grandmother lives in Kansas City and works for a greeting card company. She was watching my little brother, Chuckie, and me so Mom could go to her college teacher conference. Dad went along for the ride. "Do you think we should tell—" I began.

But Ben Benson had arrived. He pushed in front of me, then turned around. "You twerps hear about that rich guy? The land developer? He's bought the Murphy place and is building a bunch of rooms onto it."

The Murphy house was the biggest house on Cinnamon Lake. And he was building onto it?

"They say he's so rich, he's going to buy up land all over the place. Maybe turn the whole lake into a shopping mall. Or a nuclear war plant," Ben said.

Mr. Winkle drove past the bus stop, as if he'd forgotten where we get on every morning and off every afternoon. He slammed on the brakes and cranked open the door. Dirt slid ahead of Ben and Marty. I waited until the pushy kids got on. Quentin got on quietly behind me.

"Morning, Quentin," I said as I stepped onto the bus and looked around. Ben and his Vultures had their back-row seats.

"Hmm?" Quentin said. "Oh, yes."

I could almost see the gray cells turning in his brain. The science project. In all the fright of the night before, I had pushed the Junior Science Fair out of my mind. What on earth was I going to do? Today was the day we had to tell Mr. Adams about our project!

Dirt was in the second seat from the front. She was picking at something under the bus seat. I hoped it wasn't gum. I slid in beside her.

"What's wrong with you?" Dirt asked.

She hadn't even looked at me as far as I

could tell. How did she know something was wrong? "Seeing Quentin reminded me of the science fair," I explained. "I don't know what I'll tell Mr. Adams. We're supposed to know what we're doing by now."

"No sweat," Dirt said.

"No sweat for you," I said. "You don't have to stand on stage in front of the whole school and make a fool of yourself."

Dirt had succeeded in pulling whatever it was from the bus seat. Then she stuck it in her pocket. "Bugs," she said.

"Yuk!" I said. "You stuck bugs in your pocket?"

Dirt turned and raised one eyebrow at me. "No. Bugs for you."

"Thanks, but no thanks," I said.

"Molly, don't sweat your science fair project. You can use my bug collection."

"But I don't know everything about bugs like you do," I said.

"I'll tell you. You tell them. No sweat." Dirt looked out the window at the Amish plow horses turning fields into brown rows of dirt.

A bug collection. I did know more than most people about bugs. Not half as much as Dirt. But enough. Maybe. It just might work.

"And you don't mind?" I said, warming to the idea.

Dirt tilted her head to the side and frowned. She didn't mind. It was her idea. And not a bad idea at that!

We passed the Amish school. All eight grades meet in the one-room schoolhouse. Amish people live like people did a hundred years ago—no radio or TV. A little boy in Amish blues, straw hat, and bare feet waved up at us as we passed. He had a pet raccoon over his shoulders. It looked like a raccoon collar. Dirt waved back.

I looked down at Dirt's bare feet. She'd taken to carrying her shoes in her backpack. That way she could stay barefoot as long as possible. "Nobody has bugs like me," Dirt said without turning from the window.

"Thanks, Dirt," I said, wanting to say more.

Dirt shrugged. Her red cap slid down over her eyes. The cap was one of my dad's freebies. It read *Hats Off for Harry's Pizza!*

I straightened her hat. Then I remembered. *Barney's Carpet City: Throw a Whole New Light on Your Rug!* Dad's flashlight! "Oh, no!" I yelled. "Dad's flashlight! I left it in the shack!"

5

Flashlight, Flashlight! Who's Got the Flashlight?

Mr. Winkle stopped the bus so suddenly that my pack slid to the floor. "Dirt!" I yelled, grabbing my pack. "What am I going to do about Dad's flashlight?"

"Doesn't he have others?" she asked, staying in her seat.

"That's not the problem!" I said. "What if some robber lives in that shack? Remember the silverware and stuff? The police will find Dad's flashlight. Maybe they'll think Dad is the robber!"

"Move it or lose it!" someone said, bumping me hard from behind. Ben Benson. "Out of my way! I've got important people waiting."

I was standing half in the aisle. But I knew

Ben bumped me on purpose. "Watch where you're going, Ben Benson!" I called ... after he was far enough away.

Dirt darted around me and ran to the door. "No sweat!" she shouted over her shoulder. "We'll go back and get the flashlight tonight!"

I stood looking after Dirt. Go back? To that shack?

"Ahem?" Mr. Winkle had his eye on me in his rear view mirror.

"Sorry, Mr. Winkle," I said.

Just as I reached my room, the second bell rang. I started toward my desk. But *she* was in it. The new girl. I'd been so tied up with the shack monster, I'd forgotten all about what's-her-name.

"Take your seat, Molly," Mr. Adams said. He was already writing on the board.

For a minute I couldn't remember where my seat was. Then I saw Caleb. He patted the desk next to him. I slid into my new desk and tried not to look at Caleb. I tried to pay attention to the teacher. But it was no use. All I could think about was Dad's flashlight.

When I tuned into class again, Mr. Adams

was talking about the science fair. "It will be just our school," he was saying. "I thought this would be good practice for the sixth-grade science fair."

Great, I thought. We have to go through this again in three years?

"Let's hear what you all have planned," said Mr. Adams.

Quentin's hand was the first one up. "I will be building a perfect model to display barometric pressure. Secondly, I intend to disprove common theories. Thirdly, I shall—"

"Very good, Quentin," Mr. Adams said. "You may take your seat."

Quentin looked around the room and sighed, as if his genius had been wasted again. Several more kids told about their projects. Ashley had three plants, all green ferns. She'd watered one with water. Another with orange juice. And another with Diet Coke. "But you won't know what happens until the fair," she said.

A couple of the boys acted goofy, like they were dying to know what happened to the plants. "Come on, Ash," Sam said. "You can tell me. I can keep a secret."

Ashley just batted her eyelashes at him

and flipped her long blonde hair over her shoulders.

Haley wasn't about to stand for that. "Mr. Adams!" she called, waving her hand in the air. "Don't you want to know what I'm going to do for the fair?"

Mr. Adams sat on the edge of his desk. "I'm sure we'd all like to know, Haley."

"I'm showing my Aunt Mary's antique doll collection," she said.

When none of us oohed and ahhed, Haley added, "And the dress I'll wear will match her most valuable doll."

Mr. Adams rubbed his chin. "Well," he began slowly. "That sounds really ... interesting, Haley. But dolls are not exactly science, are they? What I had in mind was more—"

But Mr. Adams was stopped cold by Haley's gasp. I knew what was coming next. "You ... you ..." Haley got the words out with breathy sobs. "You ... *sob, sob* ... don't want my ... auntie's dolls?" *Sniff, sniff.*

"Well," Mr. Adams said, squirming. He dropped his red pencil. "No, Haley, I didn't mean that." He bent down to pick up his pencil.

"You didn't?" Haley asked, wiping tears

from her cheeks. "Then you *do* want my project at the fair?"

"If you can find a way to make it scientific, Haley," Mr. Adams said. "You could churn butter or demonstrate how early families—"

Haley interrupted him. "I'm sure you won't regret it, Mr. Adams. Science will be better for it."

Mr. Adams sighed weakly. He looked around the room. "Sam Benson?"

"Yes, sir," Sam said. He knew how to act like the perfect gentleman when he wanted to. "I'm going to find out, scientifically, if dogs are color-blind."

Mr. Adams nodded, like it was a good idea.

Sam went on. "I plan to set out two dog food dishes for our dog. I'll put his favorite treat in a red bowl and nothing in the green bowl. I'll do this several times. Then I'll see if my dog goes for the red bowl before he sees treats in it."

"Sounds like you have it all worked out, Sam," Mr. Adams said.

"Yes, thank you, sir," said Sam politely.

I leaned over and whispered, "Except for one small detail. You don't have a dog,

Sam Benson!"

Sam grinned at me.

"Molly?" Mr. Adams was calling me.

I straightened up in the desk. "I'm doing bugs ... I mean, showing a bug collection," I stammered.

"Uh huh?" That meant Mr. Adams wanted more.

"It will be real interesting," I promised. I tried to remember what was in Dirt's collection. "Like real ants. Fleas. Stuff like that."

A couple of girls giggled. So Mr. Adams said, "Go on, Molly. I'll bet you have a nice show planned."

"Well, yeah," I said. "Like ... how people need insects."

"Sure wish I had fleas right now," Sam whispered.

"Like ... silkworms," I blurted out. "From Japan or Korea. Someplace like that." I couldn't remember exactly. Dirt didn't have silkworms. But I wanted everybody to like my idea. "If it weren't for silkworms, they would be in trouble in those countries."

The new girl had her hand up. "Actually, it's China," she said. She turned in her seat and looked right at me. "Not Korea."

I swallowed and felt my face grow warm.

Sunny turned to the front again and went on. And on. "Silk comes from the cocoon of the silk *moth*. So it's not really a worm at all."

"The *Bombyx mori*, I believe," Quentin added.

"That's right," Sunny answered. "I can't believe you knew that, Quentin!"

Quentin beamed at her.

Sunny wasn't done yet. "The caterpillar spins a silk cocoon from its tail. It makes about 1,000 yards of silk thread. My project will also be an insect display," she said.

"Well," Mr. Adams said. "We'll all look forward to that, Sunny."

I stared at ink marks on my desk as if they were the most interesting things in the world. I had sounded so stupid. I knew it was China. Why did I say Korea?

"Mr. Adams?" It sounded like Sunny's voice, but I didn't look up. "Do these belong to someone in here? I found them in my desk. *Make your mark?*"

I jerked my head up. Sunny was reading one of my dad's pencils! To my horror, I saw her hold up one of Dad's freebie pencil sharpeners.

"This one says …" But Sunny was laughing too hard to get the words out. *"Be sharp! Shop Sharp's Auto Parts!"*

"Those are Molly's!" Sam shouted, laughing too. "Your dad made those up, didn't he, Molly?"

Sunny passed the pencil and sharpener back to me. I stuck them in my desk. They were good slogans. If Sunny hadn't made fun of them, nobody would have laughed.

"Time for recess," Mr. Adams announced.

I fiddled with my book while the room cleared.

"Aren't you coming?" Haley asked on her way out, Quentin right behind her.

"In a minute," I said.

"Boy," Haley said. "I'll bet that new girl knows as much about bugs as Dirt."

"She does seem intelligent," Quentin said. "Perhaps we should tell her about the Cinnamon Lakers."

I guess it was because she had embarrassed me in class. But I didn't like the idea. Then I felt ashamed. Sunny was new. She seemed to love nature. She was a natural for our club. "Okay," I said. "Let's ask her to a meeting."

We headed out for the playground. Sunny wasn't on the blacktop. She wasn't jumping rope.

"Oh, no!" Quentin cried. He stopped suddenly. Haley ran into him.

"What is it, Quentin?" I asked.

Then I saw for myself. Sunny was sitting on one of the swings. Behind her, pushing her gently, as nice as you please, was none other than Ben Benson!

"We really need to have a talk with this girl," I said. "About Vultures." I walked up to them. Haley and Quentin stayed put.

Sunny dragged her feet to a stop. "Hello," she said.

Ben held onto one of the swing chains. "Hi, Molly," he said. I think it was the first time Ben had called me Molly, instead of "Mack" or something worse.

"Well," I said. "I just wanted ..." Now I couldn't even talk to one person without stammering? "We have a club. The Cinnamon Lakers."

"I know," she said. She and Ben exchanged looks. Then he gave her a push that started her swinging again. I had to move out of the way.

"We just wondered," I started. But she was up, then down. I couldn't talk to her. "Hey!" I said, standing in front of her so she wouldn't swing higher.

"What's your problem?" she asked. Her voice was so harsh, I was stunned. She hopped off the swing. We were standing face to face.

"Don't bug me, Molly," she said.

And she and Ben left me standing open-mouthed.

6

Light on the Subject

"Don't bug me, Molly! That's what Sunny said, Dirt! With Ben Benson looking on and smiling as nice as you please! Like *I* was the one she had to look out for! Like I'm the one giving *her* problems!"

I'd gone home with Dirt right after class. We planned to work on the bug collection, then hunt down Dad's flashlight. We were in Dirt's room. It was so messy that at first I didn't even notice the bugs.

"You told me this about a million times, Molly," Dirt said. "Get over it. This Sunny person can't be that bad. She's cool with bugs."

Dirt brushed armloads of T-shirts and jeans off what I thought were bookshelves. Instead, she uncovered a large glass box with a lid on it. "Time to meet the guys," she said. "That's

Larry, Moe, and Curly." She pointed to three of the zillions of ants crawling in the dirt. "Ants have bigger brains than anything in the world—compared to their bodies. But you need something flashy for the science fair."

"I can't believe your mom lets you keep ants in your room," I said.

"Mom and Haley never come in here anymore," Dirt said. All over the floor were glass jars filled with dirt … and something. On the windowsill, an aquarium held flying things.

Dirt brought out bees, grasshoppers, fleas, and worms. We worked on a real show for the science project. If I could get all the facts in my head, I might have a really great project. *If* I could get the facts from my head to go out of my mouth.

"Dirt, tomorrow Mr. Adams wants us to bring in part of our fair project for practice. What should I bring?"

Dirt's eyes grew narrow. A tight smile formed on her lips. "Far out," she said. "Last night I caught something that will blow them away."

She went to her dresser and pulled out a match box with holes poked in it. Inside was a small, brownish-orange bug with black spots.

"Where'd you get it?" I asked. "It's a lady-bug, right? Did you find it around here?"

"I was down by that old shack. There it was. I call her Elaine." Dirt handed me the box.

"Thanks, Dirt," I said. "I'll be careful. I can't wait! My class will love this. I'll bet Sunny doesn't have anything like Lady Elaine."

By the time we ran Lady Elaine to my house, it was getting dark. Granny had enough food on the table to feed Chuckie, me, Dirt, and the entire state. Granny likes it when I have Dirt over. Dirt loves Granny's cooking.

"Granny," I asked between bites of fried chicken and mashed potatoes, "have you heard about that new land developer?"

"Yes," she said, spooning green beans on my plate, then on Dirt's. "Haven't seen him yet though."

"What if he builds a mall or a factory out here?" I asked. I could picture black smog hovering over our Cinnamon Lake tree house.

"Bosh!" Granny said. "He will do no such thing. Do you believe every rumor you hear,

Molly Mack? I'll bet Dirt isn't worried. Are you, Dirt?"

Dirt shrugged. What else could she do with a roll in one hand, a drumstick in the other, and a mouth full of beans?

I felt better about the land developer as Dirt and I cleared the table and got ready to head for the shack.

"You girls be careful, now," Granny said. "Wear your raincoat. You too, Dirt," she said, pushing my old poncho at her.

"Thanks, Granny Mack," Dirt said.

We made our way through the woods in the drizzle. "I don't care if I never see this shack again," I grumbled.

"Stay here," Dirt said, pushing her hood off her head. "I'll scout."

"Just hurry!" I called after her. I pulled the string of my hood tighter. The rain hid the stars and moon. I couldn't see Dirt or the shack.

Then I heard Dirt coming back. "Good news and bad news," she said. "Good news is, I found your dad's flashlight. Bad news is—there it goes now."

Through the darkness, a single beam of light flashed. It bobbed and moved away from the shack, toward the lake.

"Who has the flashlight?" I gasped.

"Follow me. We'll find out." Dirt darted from tree to tree, waiting for me to follow her.

"Dirt?" I whispered. "What are we doing?"

The light stopped moving. We tiptoed closer. A small figure in a rain poncho was bent over down by the lake. We couldn't see what the person looked like because the poncho's hood was up.

"He's got a shovel," Dirt whispered.

We watched him dig a hole. He looked all around. We held our breath. I closed my eyes. Then I heard the digging start up again.

"He's probably burying the stuff he stole," I said. "The silver and toasters and stuff."

Dad's flashlight was sitting on the ground, aimed at the hole being dug between a willow and the lake. I started to ask Dirt to move so I could get a better look at the person. But when I leaned forward to whisper at her, I stepped on a wet log. My foot slipped. I started to fall. Dirt stuck her arm out and kept me from tumbling to the ground.

But it was too late. The log crunched. The shovel stopped. The mysterious figure straightened up. As it turned our way, the hood of its poncho fell back. The flashlight shone on its face for just one second.

I let out a gasp. That face! I had seen that face before! "Run!" I told Dirt.

We galloped through the woods, through the rain, until I couldn't run any farther. Panting, I leaned against a tree. Dirt stopped beside me.

"Dirt," I said. "Did you see? Do you know who that was?"

Dirt shook her head. "I didn't get a good look."

"That ghost," I said, still panting. "It ... it was Sunny!"

7

Lady Elaine vs. Darryl

I couldn't sleep that night. Dirt didn't quite believe that I'd seen the new girl out there in the woods. But I knew what I saw. The person living in that shack and burying things in Cinnamon Lake woods was none other than Sunny!

I was so upset the next morning, I almost forgot Lady Elaine. I had to run back and get the ladybug. By the time I got to the bus, Mr. Winkle had shut the doors.

I pounded on the bus door. Finally Mr. Winkle cranked it open. I hopped on. "Thanks, Mr. Winkle," I said. "Sorry I'm late." He took off. I almost fell on Quentin's lap as I tried to take the seat behind Mr. Winkle.

"Molly," Quentin said. "As you know, I do try to sit alone. I need time to reflect. You have not forgotten about science fair rehearsal today?"

"No, Quentin. But we have a problem." I looked around to make sure nobody was listening.

"We?" Quentin said. "I am not aware of any shared problem. I have, however, observed what appears to be a matchbox on your lap."

"That's Lady Elaine," I explained. "She's not the problem. The problem is the ghost in the shack."

"Molly, I am disappointed in you. I might have expected this from Haley, but—"

"No," I said. "I know it's not a ghost."

"Well then. That's better." Quentin opened his science book.

I slammed it shut. "Quentin, listen! The person in that shack? It's Sunny! Sunny—from our class!"

Quentin frowned. "Now, Molly. I realize you two females, for some reason, are not friends. Still, you do not need—"

"I saw her!" I said. "Last night! She was burying something from the shack. Dirt and I followed her. I've been thinking. Maybe she's a runaway. Or a refugee. Or—"

"I am sure you must have been mistaken," Quentin said. "You can straighten it out in school today."

"No way!" I said. "What would I say? Besides, she'd never admit anything."

But Quentin had stopped listening. He closed his eyes in concentration until Mr. Winkle pulled into the school lot.

Inside Mr. Adams' room, everybody was hovered around Sunny's desk. If they only knew what I knew, I thought.

"Take your seats," said Mr. Adams. "This morning, you may each give us an idea of your project. Then tomorrow when you do it in the gym, you'll feel more at ease."

Most kids had interesting stuff. Ashley showed us the plant she'd been watering with Diet Coke. It was almost dead. I was getting excited to show off Lady Elaine. But before I could raise my hand, Sunny raised hers. "If you don't mind, Mr. Adams," Sunny said in a loud, clear voice. "I'd like to show the class a little demonstration."

Sunny stood in front of the class and placed a mat on Mr. Adam's desk. We got out of our seats and crowded around. Then she opened a glass jar and brought out a big, fat worm. "This is Darryl," she said.

Ashley said *yuk*. Everybody else except Haley loved it.

Sunny placed Darryl on the mat. Then she took a scissors from her pocket. Before our eyes, she cut that worm in two!

This time everybody hollered, *"Gross! Yuk! Oooh!"* Even Mr. Adams seemed grossed out. "Sunny!" he cried.

"It's okay," Sunny answered calmly. "Look." She pointed to the mat, where two

worms were now inching their way onto the desk. "Now I'd like you to meet Darryl. And this is his other brother, Darryl. Worms have several sets of organs in their bodies. So if you cut one right in the middle, both halves live. But don't do it unless you're used to worms! If you miss the middle, the whole worm could die."

All the kids clapped.

"Take your seats," Mr. Adams said. "Sunny, that was wonderful. We'll look forward to more tomorrow." When we settled down, he said, "Molly, let's see what you have for us."

I wished I didn't have to go right after Sunny. She was so good. I didn't really have a show. On the other hand, Lady Elaine was all right. In fact, she was a show all by herself.

"I brought an insect I think is really interesting," I said. "People call it a bug, but it's really a beetle." I was trying to make it longer, like Sunny's. But I guess I was getting boring. A couple of chairs squeaked. Sam yawned.

I tried to remember what Dirt taught me. "I call her Lady Elaine. And she knows how to bleed. She doesn't bleed the regular way, like we do when we get hurt. When she gets scared, she lets out drops of bloody, bitter stuff from her mouth and joints. It grosses out birds that thought they might like to eat her."

"We'd all like to meet Lady Elaine," said Mr. Adams.

I slid open the box and set the ladybug in the palm of my hand. Kids gathered around me just like they had around Sunny. Sunny was the last one to come back and look. I saw her walking toward me. For a minute I could see her face in the flashlight like it had been the night before. She was almost back to me now. She peered over Caleb's shoulder.

"What—" She swallowed whatever else she was going to say. Then Sunny gave me the maddest look I had ever seen. "Well, I wonder where you got that!" she said.

Before I could answer, she turned on her heels and clicked back to her desk.

Could Sunny have seen us spying on her the night before? I wondered. Was that why she gave me such a mean look? But why was she acting like I was the one who had done something wrong? *She* was the one hiding things in the woods. *She* was the one who wasn't who she claimed to be. I'd just have to find some way to prove it.

8

Follow That Girl!

Granny Mack had to take my little brother Chuckie to the dentist. So instead of riding the bus, I was supposed to meet them at the dentist's office at four. That gave me an hour for my secret mission. Sunny never rode the Cinnamon Lake bus. I decided to find out exactly what she did after school.

I hung around the bus as if I were going to get on. As soon as I saw Sunny, I ducked behind the tunnel slide. She waved to Ben Benson, who waved back from the bus window.

Sunny walked down the sidewalk toward Main Street. I followed, joining a group of fourth-grade girls, who acted like they couldn't talk with me around. Sunny slowed when she got to Richmond's Department

Store. She marched into the store and up to Mrs. Richmond.

I ducked below the window and peeked in. Mrs. Richmond took a red raincoat right off the window dummy and put it on Sunny. Then Sunny pulled something out of her pocket—a roll of dollar bills!

"Lose something?" It was Sam Benson! He had sneaked up behind me.

"Shhh!" I pulled him away from the window. "I'm following Sunny," I said.

"Sounds like fun. Can I tag along?" Sam asked.

"No!" I said. "Go away!"

"Thanks," Sam said, going nowhere.

Sunny was coming out. "Don't let her see you, Sam!" I whispered. Sam and I stared at cans of beans in the grocery store window. When Sunny came out of Richmond's, I was pretty sure she hadn't spotted us.

"So," Sam whispered. "You want to tell me why we're trailing Sunny?"

I started down the street after her, staying several feet back. "Listen, Sam," I said. "You know that ghost in the shack? It was Sunny." I really wanted someone to believe me. Even if it had to be Sam Benson. "I'm not kidding,"

I said. "She's living in that shack. I think she's a runaway. And now … Well, I'm pretty sure she's using stolen money to buy things."

"Wow!" Sam said, loud enough that I had to shush him again. "This is big, Molly. Maybe that's why she and my brother Ben have been such buddy-buddies."

Sunny ducked into Thompson's Hardware store.

"What's she stealing?" Sam said, chuckling. "Nails?"

But when Sunny came out, she didn't have nails. She had a bike. A brand new bike!

We spied on her in Van Kamp's Jewelry store. There, she bought necklaces, a watch, and a ring.

Then I saw the clock in the store. It was after four. "Sam! I have to meet Granny!" And I ran as fast as I could to the dentist office.

Chuckie and Granny were waiting for me. We got a quick bite at Dairy Queen. Then Granny took us home so I wouldn't miss my Thursday night Cinnamon Laker meeting.

When everybody got to our tree house, I got down to business. "I have something different planned for tonight," I said. "I know you guys don't believe that the so-called ghost of the shack is really Sunny. But it's true. She's stealing and burying the loot by the lake."

Haley laughed. "Sunny?"

Dirt shrugged.

Quentin said, "Molly, I guess you failed to work out your differences with the new girl. Still, to accuse someone of stealing requires proof."

"Exactly," I said. "And we are going to get it—tonight!"

Ten minutes and a lot of begging later, we were spying on the shack. "This isn't any fun," Haley whined. "I'm going home."

"As much as it goes against my nature," Quentin said. "I have to agree with Haley."

"No, please!" I begged. "Dirt, can you see her?"

"Nope. Probably at the digging place," she said.

"Okay," I said. "Everybody come to the spot where she buries the loot. If we don't see her, you can leave. Deal?"

They didn't want to. But they followed me. When we got to our hiding place, I was afraid it was all for nothing. Then I spotted her. "Look! She's there!"

"Are you sure that's Sunny?" Haley asked.

It was dark, and the flashlight pointed at the hole. She was wearing the old, dirty clothes, so I could understand why Haley didn't recognize her. "It's her," I said. "Just wait!"

But whatever Sunny was doing, she was done. She started walking into the woods, away from the shack.

"She's getting away!" I whispered. "Follow her!"

We trailed her through the woods. She took a dirt path and came out on the other side of the gate.

"She's headed for the Murphy place," Quentin said. "Isn't that where that rich land developer moved in?"

The front of the old Murphy house, three stories high, was flooded with light. Construction on one side of the house made a wooden shell house.

"She's going around the side!" I said.

Sunny disappeared into the darkness. She reappeared ... climbing up a ladder that leaned against the house!

"She's going to rob them!" I yelled.

"I want to go home!" Haley whined.

"It really is Sunny!" Quentin said.

"Far out!" cried Dirt. And she took off across the road after Sunny!

"Dirt! Come back!" I yelled, running after her.

Dirt stopped in the front yard. The rest of us ran up and stood next to her, watching open-mouthed as Sunny slid the second story window up and climbed inside the house! Suddenly the front door swung open. Floodlights clicked on and blinded us. "Who is out there?" came a man's voice.

"We're just kids," I said. I stepped out of the floodlight to the front walk.

The rich land developer wasn't much taller than my mom. He had red hair and was wearing a white shirt and black pants. He held a newspaper down at his side.

"I'm Molly Mack," I said. "We ... well, we saw someone breaking into your house." I felt like a tattletale for telling on Sunny. But what could I do? I couldn't just let her rob them, even if they were rich.

"Excuse me?" he said.

"What is it, Howard?" asked a woman who looked a little like him. She was pretty, with short red hair.

"I'm not sure," the man said. "These children say someone broke into our house."

She looked alarmed. "When?"

"Well … now," I said. "I mean, we saw her climb in a window on that ladder over there."

"Her?" said the man.

I nodded and looked back to Quentin and Dirt for support. Haley was gone. "I think I know who it is," I said. "She's in my class at school."

They looked at each other. Then the man seemed relieved. The woman laughed! I couldn't figure out what was wrong with them. Didn't they understand someone was robbing them that very minute?

"Sunny!" the man called out. "Come down here at once!"

Sunny! He knew about her? None of this was making sense.

Down the long staircase in the hall came Sunny, wearing muddy sweat pants. "What is it, Father?" she asked.

Father?

Then she saw me. "You!" she shouted. "What are *you* doing here?"

But I couldn't say a word.

"This young lady is reporting a robbery to

us. Have you been sneaking out collecting bugs again, Sunny?"

"Collecting bugs?" I asked weakly.

The woman who must have been Sunny's mother answered. "Sunny spends hours digging around by the lake for bugs. She's showing her collection in a science fair tomorrow." Then she turned to Sunny, who was glaring at me. "But you're in real trouble for sneaking out, Sunny. Go to your room. Your dad and I will deal with you later."

"Her dad?" I muttered. "But—"

"Can't you tell?" said her mother, fingering her husband's red hair. It looked nothing like Sunny's black hair. Then she grinned. "We adopted Sunny from Korea when she was two. She's ours, all right."

I said I was sorry and backed off the step. All the way home, Quentin and Dirt gave me a hard time. I deserved it. Why hadn't I believed good things about Sunny? Instead, because I didn't try to understand, I had believed all the wrong things.

Sunny wasn't hiding stolen goods in the shed. Her parents had so much stuff, they probably left things—like silverware and a toaster—boxed up in the shed. She hadn't been burying loot. She'd been digging for insects. Sunny hadn't stolen the money. Her parents were rich.

That night when I said my prayers, I had a lot to talk over with God. *"God, I'm really sorry. Help me to make things right with Sunny. Don't let me forget this one. Next time, help me respect people—even before I understand them. And P.S., God, will you please help me talk at the science fair tomorrow? Because if it's up to me, I'm in big trouble."*

9

On with the Show!

The next morning when I got to school, Sunny was standing on the steps with Ben Benson. Each held a box of what I supposed were Sunny's insects for the fair.

I took a deep breath and asked Jesus to help me apologize. "Sunny," I said. "I'm really sorry about last—"

She wheeled around and clutched her bugs. Without a word, she stomped into school.

Ben shook his head. "Mack," he said. "It's no use. My rich friend Sunny has heard all about you Cinnamon Lakers."

"What are you saying, Ben?"

"I told her you guys don't like her."

"Ben Benson!" I shouted, almost dropping my bug-filled basket. "Why would you tell

Sunny that?" But I already knew the answer. Ben wanted to be Sunny's only friend. And just because her family was rich!

"Well, Sunny will be waiting for these." Ben slapped the box he was holding and went inside.

Dirt plopped down on the step and pulled on her shoes.

"Oh, Dirt." I said. "No wonder Sunny hates me."

When I got to my room, it was wilder than the playground at recess. Ashley had a box of plants. Sam was sneaking a swig of her Diet Coke. Haley twirled in circles to show off her old-fashioned dress. Quentin was guarding his barometers. And Caleb had a real hunting bow with real arrows! Mr. Adams was trying to get the arrows away from him.

There was no way I could talk to Sunny. A cold sweat broke out on my forehead as I thought about all the other classes right now gathering in the gym. I set my basket on the floor and peeked in at Dirt's bugs. I asked Jesus, again, to help me.

"Class," Mr. Adams announced. "It's time to start the science fair!"

We carried our projects with us and followed our teacher to the front of the school gym. Both sides of the bleachers were filled with fourth-, fifth-, and sixth-graders. I spotted three Vultures out of the corner of my eye—Ben Benson, Marty, and Eric the Red. They were throwing paper wads at us.

The first- and second-graders sat on folding chairs in the center of the gym, leaving one side for us. We had practiced for the fair and knew which order to go in. We had to take turns sitting on stage in groups of five. My group was last.

As I sat and watched Ashley, Haley, and other kids show their science projects, I thought I might really get sick. My stomach banged together like it did when I rode the Tilt-a-Whirl at the state fair.

When it was time for my group to go on stage, Sam bounced out of the chair next to me. Kelsey, Caleb, and Sunny followed him. I stood up slowly. How could I make it to the stage when my knees kept bumping into each other?

Mr. Adams called out our names again. I sat in the last chair, next to Kelsey. I didn't know if that meant I was first or last. But the next thing I knew, Sam was walking to center stage. He set out his red and green dog dishes. Everybody listened quietly as Sam talked about Champion and how the poor dog (which he didn't have) really was color blind.

I had trouble paying attention. Sam was telling a lie, but I had done plenty of wrong things myself. And now I had to give a speech! Caleb went up and did something with his hunting bow. Mr. Adams still held the arrows, though.

Then Sunny was setting out little jars on a long folding table by the microphone. As she did it, she talked. Her voice was so loud and clear, she wouldn't have needed the microphone. "People don't give insects enough credit," she said. "Three out of every four of the world's animals are insects. There are more than one million insects for every one of us."

Sunny put on a regular bug circus. She had a jumping contest, won by the grasshoppers. A weight-lifting contest won by the ants. And when her mosquito came out as her special "blood-sucking" event, the kids cheered.

All that stood between me and center stage was Kelsey's project. Kelsey walked to the front and held up Styrofoam balls. She said they were planets. But when she tried to make them spin around the sun, Pluto and Neptune went flying off-stage into the second-graders.

I wished I could go to Neptune right then. I would go as a cockroach. Roaches could live in super freezing temperatures, and survive when it got over 120 degrees.

"Molly? Molly Mack?"

Someone was calling me back from Neptune. "You're our last science fair contestant," Mr. Adams said.

I felt frozen to my chair. Like a cockroach on Neptune. Somehow God helped me stand up, grab my picnic basket and walk to the microphone.

10

Center Stage Fright

I gazed out over the sea of elementary students. I heard chewing and popping sounds. There was a loud thumping. My own heart beating in my ears. My voice cracked when I said, "I'm showing bugs."

I couldn't believe how loud the chairs on the gym floor squeaked. How bored the first-graders looked. Everyone would rather do math drills—or dentist drills—than listen to Molly Mack.

My arms felt heavy. I'd never realized there were so many things I could do with my hands.

"Molly!" Mr. Adams whispered.

I took a deep breath. And I remembered. This seems silly, but bugs always remind me that I'm God's child. I remembered my kindergarten teacher telling us about caterpillars. She said they chewed on a leaf night and day. If a caterpillar went without food for more than a few hours, it would starve. But it didn't starve. It made a cocoon. And after a whole winter, out flew a beautiful butterfly.

I thought, If God could take such good care of a little worm and turn it into a butterfly, I knew God could take care of me. In fact, Jesus died for me and went into a grave—like a cocoon. But then He came alive again, like a butterfly. He died for my sins so I could have a beautiful new life like a butterfly. I started to feel better.

"God made every insect amazing," I said. I wasn't loud, but I could hear my voice over the microphone.

From my basket came a loud *chirp*. Dirt's cricket. I pulled the cricket jar out and held it up. "This is Jimmy Cricket," I said.

Mr. Adams stepped up for a look. "How do you know Jimmy is a boy?"

"That's easy," I answered, surprised at how regular my voice sounded. "The girls don't sing."

"All right, guys!" yelled Sam behind us.

The boys in the gym laughed. Somebody shouted, "Boys are best!"

"But boy crickets only chirp to get girl crickets. It's how they ... get dates and get married."

Now the boys settled down and girls started clapping.

"Girls really do better in the insect world," I explained. "Did you ever hear of a *king* bee or ant or termite? Only queens. The boys serve the queen."

I brought out Dirt's lightning bugs and introduced them to the audience. Again, I thought about how special God had created each insect. "These are boys." I held up the jar. "Boy lightning bugs are the ones who light up at night."

"Boys are brighter!" came a yell from the fifth-grade bleachers. I was sure it was Ben.

"The boy bugs aren't so bright," I said. "They light up to win over a girl lightning bug. But when she's done with him, she eats him! Spiders do that too. A girl black widow spider acts like she's crazy about a guy. Then she eats him. She can eat 25 boy spiders a day!"

All the girls laughed and cheered. When the noise died down, I realized an amazing thing. I, Molly Mack, was having a good time! Standing there in front of the whole school, I was enjoying myself. God cared about the insects. And He cared about *me!*

The prize of Dirt's collection was a butterfly she'd caught by the shack. She found it at the same place she'd caught the ladybug. I'd show them Dirt's prize butterfly and sit down.

"I've saved the best for last," I announced. Carefully, I lifted the butterfly jar out of the basket. "This is my Monarch—"

"That's *my* butterfly!" Sunny was out of her seat and heading for me.

"Is not!" I yelled back.

"Is so!" she screeched.

I jerked the jar away from her. My elbow rammed the display table. Then everything happened in slow motion. The whole gym fell silent for endless seconds. The table, loaded with our insects, wobbled and crashed to the ground.

Three jars rolled offstage and down to the gym floor. The first-graders were the first to jump up screaming. "Help!" cried a little boy. "Black widow's trying to eat me!"

"Don't step on them!" Sunny shouted.

The little kids started crying. Some of the girls screamed. Our principal waved madly in the air at the mosquitoes. "Go to your classes!" he said into the microphone.

I saw Dirt crawling in the bleachers, trying to capture escaped insects. I fell to my hands and knees and picked up Lady Elaine.

Sunny and I were the only ones left on stage. She tried to scoop a handful of ants into a plastic bag full of dirt.

"Why did you say the butterfly was yours?" I asked.

"Because it is! When Ben told me you stole my Monarch, I didn't want to believe it."

"Wait a minute," I said, tightening the lid on a cracked jar. "What did you say? What did Ben say?"

"That you were the one who stole my butterfly from the shed."

But I didn't," I said. "Dirt found this butterfly fair and square."

"Like she *found* my ladybug?" Sunny said. Her hands were full of worms she'd picked off the floor.

We stopped and stared at each other. "You mean," I said, "somebody took your ladybug and your butterfly—this butterfly—from the shed?"

"Come on, Molly," Sunny said. "Admit it. I found your flashlight in the shed. Ben said you were the one—"

"Ben again," I said. It was all starting to make sense. "Sunny," I said sitting on one of the folding chairs that had been flung to the front. "What else did Ben Benson tell you?"

As Sunny talked, we figured it out. Ben Benson had let Sunny's bugs loose and blamed us. He had lied to Sunny all along so he could be her only friend. He had even started rumors about Sunny's dad building a shopping mall. Sunny said her dad would never do that.

We were sitting together now. "Sunny," I said. "I'm sorry."

Sunny looked up quickly from the ladybug she'd been trying to trap under her chair. "But it wasn't you, Molly. It was Ben all along. I'm sorry I didn't know it."

"No," I said, asking God to give me the right words. "Not for that. I didn't show you much respect. I figure if God goes to so much trouble caring for bugs, He'll help me go to more trouble caring for people. I didn't even try to understand you."

Sunny smiled at me. We both had bugs crawling in our laps, trying to get out of our hands. "Molly," she said. "If that invitation to a Cinnamon Laker meeting still stands, I'd love to come."

11

The Mighty Bugs

Quentin, Dirt, and even Haley were glad to see Sunny walk up with me to our tree house. Sunny shared my branch for the whole meeting. When we were done, she said, "I think we should pay the Vultures a little visit."

"Cool," Dirt agreed.

It didn't take the five of us long to work up a plan. Sunny said she had everything we needed stored in her bug shack. We followed her there and rummaged through boxes.

"Dad bought this lot and the shack to have someplace to put our extra junk." She pulled a bag out of a crate. "Here they are!"

We examined the rubber worms and plastic insects. They almost looked real. We stuffed our pockets with the creatures and headed for the Vulture clubhouse.